Camp Girl

Camp Girl

Liz Mac

This book may be ordered through booksellers or by contacting:

iGlobal Educational Services, LLC
13785 Highway 183, Suite 125
Austin, Texas 78750
www.iglobaleducation.com
512-761-5898

Camp Girl by Liz Mac

ISBN-13: 978-1-944346-11-9

Dedication

I dedicate this book to all of my family.

Chapter 1

It was the second week that Camp Hayden had been open for kids' camps. Chloe hadn't visited her sister at all the first week since it was usually hectic and crazy. But today was the second Sunday of registration. If you paid attention, you could see a girl with amber hair with her mom unpacking her suitcase. Chloe never packed much so she had a medium sized suitcase with her pillow inside, along with other things. Her mom carried her sleeping bag and they walked over to the roped area that read 'Cowboy Camp'. They put Chloe's things in the roped area then went to registration. A new boy was at the front where they would receive all their information. If they'd paid, what camp she was in, who was her counselor, and any meds she needed. Since they had already paid and Chloe didn't need any meds, they were given a green sheet.

"Oh, it's the little Abbot. You've probably done all this before then, haven't you?" the staff member asked. Chloe looked a lot like her older sister but her name was also on her packet. Both Chloe and her mom nodded then walked off. They didn't need to go through any registration so they just walked up to where cowboy camp was hanging out; Cottonwood. Cottonwood was a large building where they sometimes held staff meetings. There was a small staff kitchen and lounge along with bathrooms that were in half of the building. The other half was two apartments. One for the assistant director and one for the nurse.

"Hello, welcome to cowboy camp. Have you ever been here before?" a nice girl asked. She looked about twenty maybe and was the girls' counselor for cowboy camp. Chloe nodded, being shy around kids her age and new people. There were six other girls in the room along with one boy and the boys' counselor, Joseph. Joseph had been there last year so he knew exactly who Chloe was. Cassidy had started working at camp the year her dad was laid off which was three years ago. Chloe had basically grown up here.

"She should warm up to the girls. If she needs anything, Cassidy Abbot is her older sister so just contact her. She knows most of the people here." Chloe's mom told the counselor.

"Oh! Okay. My name's Megan and I'll be your counselor." the girls smiled. Chloe smiled back.

"I'm gonna go talk to Cassidy. Have a good week, CJ." her mom said, hugging Chloe. Chloe hugged her back then her mom left to talk to Cassidy. CJ was a nickname Chloe had. It was short for Chloe Jenessa and Chloe liked it better. She sat down beside Joseph and watched as the group played Apples to Apples. Chloe and Joseph caught up but she didn't talk to any of the other campers. They were loud, outgoing, and most of the girls were wearing excessive amounts of makeup and talking about boys. Mostly celebrity boys they had crushes on but this wasn't Chloe's type of talk.

Mrs. Abbot made her way up to her middle daughter's cabin. Cassidy was helping Margo with the girls that were arriving but Mrs. Abbot was able to steal her for two minutes. Cassidy had her amber hair pulled into a ponytail and her brown eyes were full of energy and excitement. Unlike her little sister, Cassidy loved to meet new people and was extremely outgoing.

"So, Chloe is in cowboy camp this week but she's really nervous. I know that Hannah and Adrianne are going to be there but make sure you have an eye on her down at the waterfront or whenever you're around her. Just to make sure she's okay." Mrs. Abbot told her daughter. Cassidy nodded, knowing her little sister would be on the docks to swim in the morning while the main campers went for their classes. Cowboy camp rode horses in the morning then after lunch, some of the main campers would come up for their afternoon horsemanship lessons while the cowboy campers swam. Being a life-guard, Cassidy would be able to watch Chloe to see if she was alright.

"Okay." she replied to her mom. Her mom hugged her then left.

Chapter 2

The first full day at camp had begun on Monday morning.

Chloe woke up at four o'clock to the other six girls talking. They had been up for a while and wouldn't shut up about "how cute the other cowboy camper was". Another boy had come last evening for cowboy camp. He had been late because he rode the bus from his town to North Idaho. To make it easier for campers, Camp Hayden had a bus that ran about five hundred miles out of the Idaho state into Oregon and Washington. The girls had already woken up the counselor and Chloe was the last one to be woken up.

"Girls, go back to sleep. You'll wake Sierra." Megan scolded. Sierra was a volunteer wrangler which meant she would only be working here for three weeks. She slept in the bunk beside Chloe and had already made friends with her.

"Too late." Sierra groaned. The girls didn't seem to mind though and kept talking. Sierra took her sleeping bag and a blanket outside and laid them down so she could sleep better. Chloe wished she could do that too but knew she couldn't.

"Girls, if you don't go to sleep or at least stop talking there won't be smores sometime this week." Megan threatened. The girls instantly stopped talking and Megan soon fell asleep again. It took Chloe ten minutes though before she fell back asleep.

Only three hours later, Chloe was woken up by Megan. It was the actual time to wake up which meant getting ready for breakfast and feeding the horses. Chloe always loved being up at the barn and had spent many summers helping Hannah, the head wrangler, with the horses. She knew her way around camp better than most of this year's staff. Chloe quickly changed out of her pajamas and into jeans and a shirt. There was no dressing area so basically you either remember to change you underwear when you go down to swim or you wear the same pair all week. Chloe was the first one ready since all the girls needed the others to form a barrier around one while she changed. She grabbed her cowboy boots and went outside.

There was a medium sized pond a few feet away from the girls' cabin. It was man made but it was still beautiful. Across the pond was an amphitheater. On Wednesdays, the whole camp came out to the amphitheater and had camp fire. Camp fire was when the whole camp would meet in one area to sing songs then watch a skit before bed. It happened every night but it was almost always in a different area. The same thing happened in the morning after breakfast but before activities. The only difference was it was always in the same place. As Chloe climbed up a large rock beside the pond, she heard the girls inside scream. Then she heard what they were screaming about.

"Mouse!" one of them squealed. Chloe rolled her eyes. They were way too girly to survive this week. And there was no doubt she would be driven insane by the end of the week.

Chapter 3

When the campers arrived at the barn, Hannah, Lucita, Rachel, Sierra, and Luke were waiting for them. Lucita and Luke were new this year but were really good with horses. Especially Lucita. The group of seven girls and two boys walked over to them and waited for instructions.

"Hey, missy lou." Hannah smiled at Chloe. Hannah had been like another older sister to Chloe. Always looking out for her and making sure she was alright. One of the other girls, Gabrielle, must have thought she was talking to her because she pushed past Chloe and hugged Hannah.

"Hey! I missed you!" she squealed, hugging the confused wrangler. Gabrielle had been there last year but had driven the wranglers insane with her girliness. She wouldn't touch the horse because it was dirty and had pink riding gear.

"Alright, lets get started." Hannah said, pulling away from Gabrielle. Gabrielle smiled happily at everyone while Hannah reviewed barn rules. "Okay, first thing first, we need to bring some horses into grain today. Which works out perfectly because you guys can help us. Who wants to bring in Reflection?" Hannah asked. Jennifer's hand shot up. "Okay. Jenny gets Reflection. Who wants Winsome?" Lila's hand goes up. "Lila gets Winsome. How about Hoko?" Samuel's hand goes up. "Sam will get Hoko. So Lila, Jenny, and Sam go with Sierra." Hannah instructed. The three grabbed their horse's halter and followed Sierra out.

"So you all know how to halter a horse, right?" Sierra said both they were gone.

"Next is Zeus. I'm going to give him to--" Hannah was cut off by Irie, another girl like Gabrielle.

"I'll take him. He's my baby anyway." she said, looking at all the other girls. Zeus was a nine year old thoroughbred. He had just been upgraded in training from staff only horse to camper horse. He belonged to Sophia Abbot, Chloe's oldest sister, but she didn't work at camp this year so she had given him to Hannah to train. The staff had only let one camper ride Zeus so far and that was because she was a very experienced teen rider.

"Actually, Irie, I was going to give Zeus to Chloe. He is her sister's horse after all." Hannah said. Irie huffed in response and glared at Chloe. "Gabrielle, you can take

Thunder. Kyler gets Duke. Annie, can you get Snickers? Irie, grab Zippo please. And Lexi gets Smokey. Chloe come with me since Zeus is in with Red. Irie and Kyler go with Luke. Lexi and Annie go with Lucita." Hannah dismissed them and they all went to get their horse's halter.

"You better watch out, baby girl." Irie whispered in Chloe's ear. Chloe shrugged her off and grabbed Zeus' halter then went out to Hannah.

"Having fun yet?" Hannah asked.

"Yeah. But I'm hungry." Chloe answered.

"There's apples in the fridge inside the staff tack shed. Breakfast isn't for another hour so go ahead and grab one." Hannah offered. When they arrived at the corral with the rowdy dun, Hannah opened the gate. Zeus was a far size and extremely gentle horse. Even though sometimes he might throw you off by mistake. Zeus was in a special pen with Rachel's horse Red. Red was a beautiful fifteen year old Dutch Warmblood with a chestnut coat. He had a blaze down his face and a long mane and tail. Chloe walked up to Zeus who recognized her and slipped his halter on. He sniffed her pockets for treats since the Abbot girls had a habit of bringing the spoiled boy apple cores or carrots. She walked with Hannah back inside the barn and hitched him up. Hannah let her mix up his grain on her own since she knew how Sophia had it mixed. She stirred it for a little bit then clipped the bucket on the railing and let Zeus dig in.

"I'm gonna go wash my hands." Chloe told Hannah. She nodded so Chloe walked out of the barn. On the way out, she spotted Lexi and Irie talking.

"She hates getting dirty. She has to wash her hands after graining a horse." Irie snickered to Lexi. Chloe was used to this type of stuff. She rushed out and washed her hands before going back into the barn and towards the staff tack shed. Lucita just glanced as the girl walked in, knowing who she was, then went back to assigning horses for the staff trail ride on Thursday morning. When Chloe walked out with an apple, Annie gave her a questioning look. Annie wasn't rude to Chloe but she wasn't nice.

"You're not allowed in there, princess." Irie sneered.

"I am if my sister is a staff member and my other sister used to be the head wrangler. Besides, Hannah said I could get an apple if I was hungry." Chloe replied calmly.

"I doubt that. Hannah loves me the most." Gabrielle chimed in. Chloe just walked by them and went over to Zeus and Sierra.

Chapter 4

When it was time for breakfast, Adrianne, the horsemanship director, drove a small yellow bus up to the barn. It was cowboy camp's way of getting from the barn down to where the main camp was. They walked into the cafeteria and over to the table that had a sign on it for Cowboy camp. They were late so most of the camp was already there. The girls' dorm director did announcements then went to dismiss tables. Cassidy walked over to the cowboy camp table and put a chair between Chloe and Annie.

"Hey, how's the first day been so far?" she asked. Chloe laughed and she got a glass of water.

"It's breakfast, Sid." Chloe answered. "But it's fine."

"That's not a very happy fine." Cassidy debated. Chloe just looked at her.

"It's breakfast. Wait until maybe tomorrow to ask that." she replied. "Aren't you supposed to be with Margo?" she asked. Cassidy pointed her finger at her.

"Supposed to be. Not have to be." she pointed out. Chloe rolled her eyes but Irie was wondering why such a girl like Cassidy would want to hang out with Chloe. "You wanna introduce me to your friends or no?" Cassidy asked.

"Oh! Sure. That's Hannah and Sierra's over--"

"No. I mean your camper friends." Cassidy interrupted. **I don't have any,** Chloe thought. But she just smiled.

"That's Irie, Annie, Gabrielle, Lexi, Lila, and Jenny. Girls, this is Cassidy." Chloe said.

"You are so pretty! How did you get your hair like that?" Gabrielle asked Cassidy.

"I was born with it this way." she answered. Gabrielle, Irie, Jenny, and Lila started to talk about hair while Annie and Lexi talked to Cassidy. Chloe just drank her water then they were dismissed. "Are they always like this?" Cassidy whispered to Chloe. She nodded and Cassidy said, "Ouch." They get dismissed to go get their breakfast so they get up and go stand in line.

"Hey, girls!" Sierra smiled, hopping in line behind Chloe and Hannah. She had a happy look on her face and was smiling like an idiot. Hannah and Chloe shared a knowing look then looked at Sierra.

"What happened? Why are you so happy?" Hannah asked.

"Is it Asher?" Chloe questioned. Sierra glared at Chloe who just smiled.

"For your information, yes. Asher asked me out!" Sierra squealed. Hannah and Chloe laughed as they got their food and Sierra kept talking about Asher. She's had a huge crush on him for forever. Breakfast was waffles with fruit sauce and sausages. Chloe and Cassidy both got their fruit sauce in a seperate bowl so they could put peanut butter on their waffles first. After getting their waffles and sausages, they went out to the condoments bar and spread peanut butter on their waffle. When they got back to their table, they put the fruit sauce on their waffle and drizzled some syrup on their sausages.

"You girls are twins." Hannah stated as she watched them both do the same thing.

"No, we're not." they both answered. The campers were confused as to why they both acted the same way, looked alike, and talked at the same time. It only clicked in the boys' brains because the other girls were too anit-Chloe to realize that she was sisters with this girl named Cassidy. When Cassidy finished her food, she got up from the table and threw her plate away.

"Well, I have to go. Duty calls." she tells Chloe and Hannah. Chloe had seen her look over her shoulder and spotted Jason Hayes across the room.

"Don't you mean Jason calls?" she teased. Cassidy playfully slapped Chloe's head then walked away. "Love you too." Chloe mumbled. Cassidy went over to Jason and they went down to the dock to organize for the campers.

"Alright girls, we're going back up to the barn then we are going to come back down here and swim for the morning. Any questions?" Megan asked.

"Do we have to swim? Can we just talk?" Lila asked.

"Sure." Megan nodded. Chloe rolled her eyes. She was sure that if the girls were allowed to bring nail polish, they would be painting their nails and gossiping about cute boys instead of swimming. Who was she kidding? They were going to gossip about boys anyway.

Chapter 5

As they arrived at the beach, they all got out of the bus carrying their swim suits and towels. The girls were gossiping about celebrities and the boys weren't paying attention to anyone or anything. Chloe set her towel on the picnic tables by the store along with everyone else and left her flip-flops up there too. Megan told the girls to wait to get in the water until they had a lifeguard in the swim area. The girls followed her to the dock and sat on the edge with their feet in the water once Megan had gotten a lifeguard for them. It just so happened to be Jason. Chloe dove into the water, accidently splashing all the girls who screamed as if they were being attacked by a serial killer. When Chloe resurfaced, all the girls were glaring at her and Jenny yelled at her.

"You idiot! You know how much this swim suit cost?" she asked.

"Five bucks?" Chloe guessed.

"No! One hundred dollars!" Jenny answered. **Who buys a swim suit for a hundred dollars and doesn't swim in it?** Chloe thought. She swam over to Jason who wasn't really paying attention. He was watching Cassidy teach some kids who to wakeboard. Chloe jumped out and sat beside him.

"Just marry her already." she stated. Jason jumped at the sound of Chloe's voice and glared down at her.

"You scared me, Abbot." he replied. Cassidy and Jason had been dating for three years but had known each other since Chloe was born. The boy with dirty blonde hair and blue eyes had instantly drawn Cassidy to the Hayes family, which meant Chloe had known them all her whole life. Jason was like a brother. "And I was planning on it, genius." he told her.

"Really?!" Chloe smiled hugely. Jason rolled his eyes.

"Yes. But you better not ruin it. So keep your mouth shut, Chloe." he answered. Chloe nodded before pretending to zip her mouth shut, lock it, and throw the key in the lake.

"CJ, can you grab the blue rope in the boat house?" Cassidy asked. Chloe got up and went into the boat house. She grabbed the blue wakeboard rope then handed it to Cassidy. "Thank you. Did you put on sunscreen?" Chloe shook her head. Cassidy shoved her back towards the boat house where Chloe found sunscreen and put it on.

"CJ? That sounds like a boy's name. She must have thought you were a boy and I can see that happening." Gabrielle snarled. Chloe ignored her and went over to Jason. But by the end of the week, if this didn't stop, she knew she'd have trouble.

After lunch, they had rest period for an hour at cowboy camp. Rest period was where the campers and staff have one hour to rest or prepare for their next class. Chloe was in the cabin drawing and so were the other girls. But Megan wasn't in the cabin which meant it was only Chloe and the girls. She was drawing a picture for Cassidy's birthday next week and she had been working on it for a couple days now. It was a picture of Cassidy and Jason. She had a picture of them together laying in a field so she decided to draw it. She was a great artist and was always proud of her work. Then Irie and Gabrielle came over.

"Whatcha drawing?" Irie asked.

"It looks like her and her boyfriend." Gabrielle chimed in.

"Come on, Gabby. This is Chloe we're talking about. She doesn't have a boyfriend. Only pity parties." Irie said. Gabrielle and Irie laughed and Chloe tried to ignore them but she couldn't just block her mind. When she was drawing, she needed her mind open so she couldn't close it up and keep drawing. All the girls started teasing her about her drawing so Chloe got up and ran outside.

She climbed on top of a rock the overlook the pond. She held her art book close before going back to drawing. These girls were bullying her and she didn't like it. **I can make it to the end of the week though,** she told herself.

Chapter 6

At the barn, everyone was paired up for grooming horses. It was Jenny and Annie, Sam and Kyler, Gabrielle and Lexi, Irie and Lila, and Chloe was with Luke, a wrangler. Chloe grabbed a curry comb, hard brush, soft brush, and hoof pick. When she reached Zeus, Chloe ducked under the rail and started on the curry comb. Rubbing it in circles against Zeus's coat, she quickly finished with the curry comb before Irie had the chance to even get back and duck the rail.

"Geek." Irie mumbled, loud enough for Chloe to hear, as she passed. Chloe moved around to the other side and finished just as quick. Then she took both the hard brush and the soft brush, each in a different hand, and started on the left side. Flicking the hard brush then running the soft brush over the area, Chloe used both hands to groom Zeus. Luke was just standing by and watching her while Chloe grabbed Zeus's foot and took out all the gunk. Zues was fully done and Chloe was reaching for his saddle and bridle in the tack shed. She carried it out to Zeus and hung the bridle on the rail and rested the saddle on top of it while she flipped the saddle pad on Zeus. Then she chucked the thirty pound saddle on him like it was nothing. She cinched him up and slipped his bridle in. She was done with everything in less than six minutes. Hannah walked over and gave Chloe a high five.

"You've learned well, young one." she said.

"I learned from the best two girls." Chloe replied, referring to Hannah and Sophia. Hannah pushed her head away playfully then they both went over to the staff tack shed and got an apple. They both sat on the hay bales and ate their apples while waiting for everyone else. When they were, they walked over in front of Hannah, the girls too worried about their outfits to sit on anything.

"Alright, we've got riding tests to take then classes. Everyone grab a helmet, yes we spray them after every use, then come out to the arena." Hannah instructed. Chloe grabbed her helmet from the staff tack shed and the everyone else grabbed one to borrow. Irie walked over to Chloe, seeing her nice helmet, and stood in front of her.

"I want your helmet. Give it to me." she commanded.

"No way. It's mine." Chloe replied.

"No, it's the camp's. Now give it to me." Irie demanded.

"No, it's not the camp's. I bought it." Chloe told her. Irie rolled her eyes and walked off. Chloe knew exactly how the ride test went. Even though she had never been a cowboy camper, she had helped give ride tests with Hannah last year. A highlight of her oldest sister running the horsemanship. However, she wasn't there this year.

"Sierra's going to show you how the ride test will go. We'll watch you ride and then put you in classes designed to your own level." Hannah told them. Sierra rode around three barrels then went into a keyhole made by cones and walked over two three inch tall poles that were lay- ing on the ground. "Next, if you want, you can trot. If you trot, you can chose to gallop after that of not. It's entirely up to you. Who's first?" Irie got up and walked inside the arena. Hannah had to help her up into Birdie and Rachel wrote down how well she did. After missing every bar- rel, knocking down some cones, and hitting the poles, Irie wasn't doing very well even though she felt proud. **There is no way Chloe is better than me,** she thought.

"Can I trot now?" she asked, gleefully. The wranglers looked at each other and shook their heads.

"No. Next." Rachel said as Hannah helped Irie off. Next was Gabrielle. She only did a little better and fell off while trotting. She started crying and Megan had to take her up to the cabin. Then it was Jenny's turn. She was good. She got all the barrels, but knocked down cones, missed the poles, and didn't trot. Annie did great.

She did everything but gallop. Then it was Sam. Both the boys did good but they needed to work on their trot. Lexi and Lila were both as bad as Gabrielle except they didn't fall or trot. Then it was Chloe's turn. She was last. She mounted Birdie quickly and went around the barrels, not hitting a single cone, and going over the poles perfectly. Hannah smiled and gave her a nod. Chloe started in a trot around the large arena and after going around once, she asked Birdie to gallop. Birdie recognized her signal instantly and went into a smooth gallop around the arena. All the campers were watching her in awe while Hannah smiled aprovingly. Birdie stopped as soon as Chloe asked her to then Chloe dismounted perfectly.

"Beautiful, CJ." Hannah told her. Chloe walked towards the exit and all the campers went to a grassy area to wait while the wranglers assigned them horses and classes.

Chapter 7

When the wranglers returned, they had everything planned out. Chloe made it harder for them though. She was the most advanced and no one else was at her level. So they would put Irie, Gabrielle, Lila, Jenny, and Lexi in a group. Then Sam, Kyler, and Annie would be a group and lastly, Chloe would be with Hannah and have her own lesson. After telling the campers this, they split up in their groups. Gabrielle, Irie, Jenny, Lila, and Lexi went into the barn with Luke and Sierra while Sam, Kyler, and Annie went with Rachel and Lucita to get their horses then into the trail arena. The trail arena was half as big as the main arena but would work well for their class. Chloe got Fancy, Rachel's horse, and then followed Hannah out to the big arena. Fancy was in an English saddle but Chloe could ride English just as well as Western. Hannah had turned the poles into small jumps for Chloe. Chloe mounted Fancy after checking her cinch and Hannah walked to the center of the arena.

"Alright. Ready to start jumping?" she smiled.

"No way!" Chloe gasped. She had always wanted to learn how to jump but Sophia was too busy with college and work and Cassidy didn't know a thing about horses. Her brother, Perry, didn't know anything about horses and was the only Abbot who hadn't worked at camp. He was a video game specialist and the oldest of the four.

"Yep. Sophia told me you wanted to learn so, I pulled some strings and now you get to learn." Hannah replied. "So you start out by galloping around the arena."

After classes, it was dinner time. Chloe was still happy about her private lesson with Hannah. She had fallen off Fancy twice but was okay both times. Then she finally made it over to jump and was ecstatic. So was Hannah. She was proud she could be the first one to see her make it over a jump and teach her how to do it. So both the wrangler and the camper had smiles on their faces when they arrived at the cafeteria with Adrianne and the other cowboy campers. The other girls hadn't had as great of a time. They spent the day learning how to start, stop, and turn their horses. Then the group that had gone to the barn, had spent the whole time in the barn. Each class would have two days of riding and one day of barn work.

"What's all the smiley smiley about?" Cassidy asked as she plopped down in a seat by Chloe. An empty seat beside Cassidy was soon filled by Jason.

"Hannah taught me to jump! I fell twice but then I made it over." Chloe gushed. Irie, Gabrielle, and Jenny rolled their eyes.

"Wait, and you didn't die?" Jason questioned before taking a sip of water. Chloe glared at him.

"No." she replied.

"I'm so proud of you! Wait until I tell Phia!" Cassidy said. Phia was the nickname they had both given Sophia when they were little even though that was a six year difference.

"No! I want to tell Phia." Chloe argued back.

"Maybe I already told Phia." Hannah butted in. Both girls gaped at her and she laughed. "I'm kidding." Hannah told them.

"Dibs on telling Sophia." Chloe muttered to Cassidy. Cassidy crossed her arms and pouted. "That only works on Jason." she reminded her. Jason opened his mouth to object then realized it was true. The girls' director did announcements then went around dismissing tables.

"Hey, who are you?" Irie asked Jason flirtously. Cassidy and Chloe tried to hide their laughter, Cassidy had a harder time though. This twelve year old girl couldn't date her boyfriend anyways so why get defensive?

"Jason." he replied, unsure of what to do. He looked at Cassidy who just smiled and motioned for him to continue the act. "Who are you?" he asked. Not flirtously though.

"Irie Jennings. You are really cute. How old are you?" she asked.

"Um, thanks? And I can't tell you my age. Camp rules." Jason answered. "And you're twelve. I'm way to old for you."

"So? No one has to know." Irie told him. Hannah, Cassidy, and Chloe all burst out laughing and Jason looked around confused. Irie's face flushed in embarressment and she slumped down in her seat. Cassidy threw her arm around Jason and Chloe caught a glint of some shiny object out of the corner of her eye. Closer examination told her it was a ring on her left ring finger.

"Honey, he's my boyfriend." Cassidy told her.

"I'm sorry." Irie mumbled. Chloe leaned over and whispered in Cassidy's ear.

"I'm gonna pretend I didn't see that ring." she whispered. Cassidy turned and faced her then showed her the ring.

"I love it." she told her sister. Hannah looked over and saw the ring then gave Cassidy a look. Cassidy nodded and Hannah smiled.

"Nice, Jason." she stated.

Chapter 8

The rest of the week, Chloe had mixed feelings. She was happy that she had private classes and that her sister was engaged to one of her best friends but Irie, Jenny, and Gabrielle were constantly bullying her. She was trying to ignore them but the more they did it, the more she thought it might actually be true. It was Thursday evening and they were getting ready for a long trail ride out into the woods. Every Thursday, the cowboy campers rode out in a single file line with some wranglers to a place out in the woods. They would be spending the night out there on tarps in their sleeping bags and the horses would be tied to the high-line. The high line was a rope stretched across fifty feet of grass between two trees where they tied to lead ropes in order to keep the horses in one place.

"Alright, everybody ready?" Hannah asked. Only half of the group would ride out there. The other half would ride back. Since there were only nine campers, the four best riders would ride out there since the trails wasn't for beginners, then the other five would ride on the way back Friday morning. It was basically flat on the way back. Chloe, Sam, Kyler, and Annie were riding out. Hannah was leading on Red, then Chloe on Zeus, Sierra on Luna, then Sam on Snickers, Kyler on Hoko, Rachel on Fancy, Annie on Thunder, then Lucita in the back on Star. Adrianne and Luke were driving the other five and Megan out to the campsite.

"Yep." they all replied. Hannah started Red and the rest followed him. The ride would be about an hour but Chloe knew better than to think it would be boring. She went on these rides every week with her older sister in previous years so she knew the trail just as well as Hannah. They had even invented a game that Hannah had taught the other wranglers the first week of camp. Twiggy.

"I'm starting Twiggy!" Hannah exclaimed about fifteen minutes into the ride. She took a small twig from a tree and they kept walking forward. When she found a good place, she put Twiggy there. Chloe had to remember where Hannah had set Twiggy and picked him up. Twiggy had to be set in other branches so you could reach him from your horse. Then Chloe found a spot for Twiggy. Then it was Sierra's turn. Sierra explained the game to

Kyler and Sam then they joined in. Rachel explained the game to Annie and Twiggy made it all the way to the back of the line with Lucita.

"Twiggy lived!" Lucita said. The wranglers passed the message up until it reached Hannah. They played this for about half an hour until most of the Twiggy's had done flips off branches and died or made it to the back of the line. They were five minutes out from where they were going to arrive when Hannah looked back at Chloe and gave her a look. Chloe knew what it meant and smiled widely. Her and Sophia had started this and Hannah had picked up on it. They were the only three that did it but they loved it. Sierra had seen the look Hannah gave Chloe and knew that some crazy thing was about to happen. And boy was she right.

I'm a little pile of tin, nobody knows what shape I'm in.
I got four wheels and a running board,
I'm a four door, I'm a Ford.
Honk, honk, rattle, rattle, rattle, crash, beep, beep.
Honk, honk, rattle, rattle, rattle, crash, beep, beep.

Both Hannah and Chloe sang loudly. Sierra joined in the second round and then all the wranglers were singing with them. When they arrived, they were still yelling it but Annie, Sam, and Kyler just looked at them like they were insane. They stopped and the wranglers dismounted before holding the horses so the campers and Chloe could get off. They tied the lead ropes to the high-line and untacked the horses. Chloe slipped the bridle off and threw it over her shoulder. Then pulled off the saddle and pad and walking over to the board where she laid them. Then she went over to where Adrianne was unloading the wrangler truck and the girls were setting out there beds. Chloe found her stuff chucked out of the way so she picked it up and walked over to the edge of the tarp. Except, the girls were taking the whole width. Chloe put her sleeping bag on the second tarp between the bench and where Adrianne would sleep. Adrianne would be closest to the fire and the other girls were far from it because she didn't want any of them to get burned on accident.

"How was the ride over?" Adrianne asked, putting her sleeping bag beside Chloe's.

"Interesting. We played Twiggy when sang *I'm A Little Pile of Tin*." Chloe answered. They walked back over to the main fire where they would be eating and hanging out until bed time. Adrianne got out the food and they started eating as soon as all the wranglers were back. After they ate, everyone just hung out and talked for hours and hours until it was dark. Hannah looked at Adrianne who sighed and nodded.

"Okay, who wants to hear a story?" Hannah asked. Chloe had heard the story a zillion times, considering it was her sister who made it up when a camper kept walking into one Birdie's corral without permission. "So, once there was a counselor here named Bernadine. This was back when Adrianne and I were campers but Birdie was here. Bernadine was great with horses, in fact, she was the best wrangler up here. When we went on the over nighter my second year of camp, Bernadine offered to sleep by the horses like Sierra and I are going to do. So, we all went to sleep and Bernadine went out to the horses. But in the middle of the night, nobody knows how, but the high-line broke and Birdie started to freak out. Bernadine woke up and tried to calm down Birdie but got kicked and instantly died. We buried her where the pond now is up at cowboy camp since a corral used to be there and she always wanted to be with horses. But my first year as a wrangler up here, I was walking by the pond in the morning and I saw her. Bernadine was running across the pond towards me. Bernadine was running across the pond towards me. As soon as she touched land though, she disappeared. She's been spotted by many campers ever since and her things have been disappeaing without explanation. Like her saddle, just before you guys came to camp this week, her saddle went missing but all the was found on the security cameras was the saddle floating away as she carried it with her." Hannah said. The girls were holding onto each other, scared out of their minds knowing Birdie had come on the trip with them.

"Is it real?" Lila asked. Hannah nodded, trying to hide her smile.

"That's terrifying." Lexi whispered.

"I have a warning for you guys. If you see any greenish glowing light, don't follow them. You know the lights in Brave that lead Meredith to the witch's house? Yes, they haunt these woods and if you follow them, they'll lead you to your death. Never follow the lights." Joseph warned. The girls were about to cry they were so scared. But what they didn't realize was that Luke wasn't with them. He had left in the middle of the Bernadine story and was creeping up behind them. Chloe saw him and told Hannah. Then Luke came running out of the woods. He yelled and everyone screamed. Even the wranglers except Hannah and Chloe who were laughing so hard they were holding their stomachs.

"Ahh!" Adrianne screamed. The girls started crying and Megan was trying to comfort them.

"Alright. No more stories or scaring. Bed time." Megan told everyone. They made their way back to their sleeping bags and as soon as Chloe's head hit the pillow, she was out.

Chapter 9

The next morning, they had breakfast then packed everything up in the wrangler truck. Irie, Gabrielle, Jenny, Lila, and Lexi all got on a horse and they started back while the others packed up. Then they loaded the small yellow bus and Adrianne drove them back to cowboy camp while Megan drove the wrangler truck. Chloe had already started believing the things the girls were telling her and it took everything in her not to cry when she thought about it. Hannah had noticed Chloe wasn't herself and notified Cassidy. However, they wouldn't see Cassidy until after campfire that night because it was her day off. Even if Chloe was her happy self yesterday, that day had come and gone and she was back to being upset. Especially after "that stunt she pulled on the overnighter", the girls had been rude. By the time they were all back and the horses were all taken care of, it was lunch time. Today cowboy camp wouldn't ride horses they would swim in the afternoon with no riding. Lunch was terrible since Hannah wasn't there and the girls kept whispering mean things to Chloe. After lunch, they had rest period in Cottonwood and waited for the dock to open. When it did, they could go swimming. They changed when classes started and they could finally swim. Chloe was the first one changed and she went out to the dock where Joseph and his two boys were. She didn't see Jason since it was also his day off. The likelihood was that both Cassidy and Jason were across the bay in the lake house.

"Hey, Chloe." Joseph smiled.

"Hey, Joseph." Chloe replied. Lila came up behind Chloe and pushed her into the water. Chloe, not having expected that, forgot to hold her breathe and got water up her nose before she could resurface. When she did, the lifeguard was glaring at her. Lila had pushed her in before there was a lifeguard which meant that Chloe couldn't swim for the rest of the week since she had "jumped" in.

"Get out. You can't swim for the rest of the week." Will told her. Chloe got out and sat on the edge of the dock.

"But I was pushed in. Lila pushed me and Joseph saw it." she defended. Will looked at Joseph and he nodded. Then he looked at Lila.

"No horseplay. If it happens again, you can't be on the dock." Will warned. After that, Chloe just sat on the dock with her feet dangling in the water. The day went by slowly for Chloe but too quickly for Cassidy and Jason. They were hanging out in the beach house for the day. In fact, they had even taken Jason's boat over. They could see camp easily from the house and Chloe could see the beach house.

"It's already time for campfire. We need to head back." Cassidy told Jason, looking at the big clock in the living room. Their day off ended Friday night campfire and they needed to be back by the end of it. Jason groaned loudly and rolled off the couch. Cassidy grabbed her phone from its charger and checked it. She had left it alone all day and ignored all notifications but when she saw a text from Hannah about Chloe, she read it instantly. **Hey, Chloe needs you. She isn't herself** the text read. "Jason, move faster! I have to get to Chloe." Cassidy yelled as she ran down to the dock. Jason ran after her and started the boat. They drove over to the camp dock and Jason could barely park the boat before Cassidy leaped out.

"Okay, what even happened to Chloe?" Jason asked.

"I don't know. Hannah just texted me and said she wasn't herself." Cassidy answered.

"Well it won't help if you kill yourself trying to get there." he replied. Cassidy rolled her eyes and she saw the Cottonwood light on. As they climbed the stairs, she looked in Cottonwood and saw cowboy camp in there so they went inside. As soon as they did, the girls raced over and Irie, Gabrielle, and Lexi started flirting with Jason while Lila and Jenny talked to Cassidy. Annie was talking to Sam. Cassidy saw Chloe in the corner reading something on paper so she walked over to her and sat beside her. Chloe folded the letter back up and put it in the envelope in came in. Her mom had sent her a letter at dinner today.

"What's wrong?" Cassidy asked.

Chapter 10

Chloe shrugged. She didn't want to talk about this here, with the girls around. Cassidy grabbed her hand, pulled her up, then walked into the empty staff kitchen and shut the doors. Then she turned to Chloe and crossed her arms.

"Tell me." she commanded.

"It's nothing. The girls have just been really rude to me. They keep bullying me and telling me I'm stupid, an idiot, that I'm being babied by the wrangler's because my sister works here, and everything else. It's been the worst week ever." Chloe cried. Tears came out of her eyes and Cassidy hugged her. She tried comforting her but it didn't work. Her little sister always believed what people said even if they weren't telling the truth and that was something Cassidy couldn't stop. She pulled away from Chloe and poked her head out of the kitchen.

"Jason!" Cassidy called. He looked up and walked thruogh the swarm of girls. Cassidy grabbed his wrist and pulled him into the kitchen, locking the girls out. They immediately objected to the shutting door, saying that they had the right to know what happened to Chloe since they were all friends. But Cassidy knew that was a lie.

"What's wrong, CJ?" Jason asked.

"The girls bullied her all week." Cassidy answered. She hugged Chloe again and Jason walked out.

"He's gonna kill them all." Chloe mumbled. She and Cassidy started laughing and Chloe dried her tears. Cassidy got her a cold, wet cloth to wipe her face with, and then they exited the kitchen to find Jason. All the girls were in the corner whispering while Jason was talking with Megan and Joseph.

"The biggest lie in every school and camp is that bullying won't be tolerated. So prove that to the girls and give them a punishment." Jason said. Irie and Gabrielle gasped.

"But JayJay, why would you want us in trouble?" Gabrielle asked. Jason pointed to Chloe who's face was still red.

"That." he said. Cassidy calmed him down and told him to leave, which he did, while she took care of it.

"I'm just gonna take her out of camp for the rest of the week. She's no longer a camper." Cassidy said. Megan nodded as Hannah walked into Cottonwood.

"Who's no longer a camper?" she asked. Chloe raised her hand. "Why? What happened?"

"The other girls bullied her so she's just gonna hang with me. It just means we start our summer hang out two days sooner." Cassidy shrugged.

"Okay. Come up Monday, CJ." Hannah whispered in her ear. Chloe nodded then followed Cassidy outside and up to the road that went through camp. They walked to Jason's cabin and banged on the door. He opened it up in his pajamas and looked at them.

"What?" he asked.

"We're stealing your hammock, okay? Okay! Thank you!" Cassidy smiled. He turned around, picked up his hammock that was rolled up, and chucked it at her.

"You want Shawn's too?" he asked. Shawn was his older brother. He didn't work at camp but had given Jason his hammock for the summer so that if he broke his own hammock again, he could use Shawn's. Cassidy nodded so he chucked Shawn's hammock at Chloe.

"Thank you?" Chloe said, although it sounded like a question.

"See yah later, Jason." Cassidy waved as both she and Chloe went back down to the beach. There was a row of girls' dorms for the female staff but they were always full since there were only eight of the cabins and they were pretty small. So most of the girls put hammocks in between the sixteen poles that held up the three story building. Cassidy had her hammock tied up so they had an extra hammock. Well, it would have been extra if Ariana wasn't using it. So they tied the two hammocks up then Cassidy got two pillows and two blankets for them sine it got cold at night. They got in the hammocks and were quickly asleep.

The next morning after breakfast, Cassidy and Chloe had Adrianne drive them up to cowboy camp during camp counsel so Chloe could get all her stuff. They rolled up her sleeping bag, grabbed her pillow, threw her swim suit and towel in her suitcase, then packed everything up in the yellow bus and drove back down before activities started. Saturday was a different schedule than the other days. Each cabin was in a team for the Amazing Race. For example, the cabin G6, girls' dorm 6, and B6, boys' dorm 6, would be one team. Same with all the other numbers. They would travel all over camp, up to cowboy camp, and down to the docks, to do activities and get clues. The team with the most clues and the correct answer to a quiz question won and got to swim in the pool that night. Wakeboard camp would be split into two boats then pass out cookies to people who were out on their docks around the lake. Cowboy camp would be a team in the Amazing Race. Cassidy and Chloe carried Chloe's stuff down to Cassidy, Ariana, and soon-to-be Margo's cabin and put her bags in there. They traded the blanket in Chloe's hammock for her sleeping bag then she used her own pillow.

"So, to the dock?" Chloe asked Cassidy. She shook her head.

"Nope. Wakeboard camp doesn't go out until after lunch. They'll be playing mind games and other things in Cottonwood until then. You, Jason, and I get to make the batter then bake two hundred cookies in two hours." Cassidy said. They met up with Jason in the kitchen where they found he had the recipe for a dozen chocolate chip cookies.

"We'll triple the recipe and each of us will make our own batter. So three batches of 36 cookies equals about one hundred and eight cookies. So we'll do that twice. Ready, set, go!" Jason yelled. The kitchen staff looked at them weirdly but they raced to get huge bowls and then did the math to triple the recipe.

Chapter 11

They had barely taken the last batch of cookies out of the giant ovens when the kitchen staff started to use them. There were four large ovens and they had needed to use all of them in order to be done in time. They kept the cookies on the baking sheets in the kitchen office so they could cool off and not be in the way. They also put signs up to tell the staff they couldn't have any of the cookies yet. Then they went to go get lunch. Most of the support staff weren't sitting with their cabins since it was Saturday and usually, quite a few campers' families came to visit. So they sat with Ariana, Hannah, Christian, and Sierra in the ping pong room to the side of the cafe. There were two tables set up and they had set up chairs.

"Hey, Ari, this is my baby sister Chloe. Chloe, this is Ariana but we all call her Ari." Cassidy introduced to two. Chloe had met Christian a few years ago when he first started working at camp with Hannah. They had been dating for three years as well as having grown up together.

"Hey." Chloe waved. Then it was chaos. Being college students, not very responsible ones at that, they were all talking over each other and trying to reach the water or salt from across the table. It was a loud room and as more people came in that Chloe met, the louder it got. Then a very familiar brunette cowgirl walked in with a visitor's pass hanging from her belts loops and it got quiet for a split second and then, "Phia!" Chloe yelled. She hadn't seen her older sister since school started. Cassidy had seen her every now and then since they went to the same college but rarely. So Hannah, Sierra, Cassidy, Chloe, Rachel, and Lucita all got up and jumped over to hug her.

"Wait! Let me put my food down." Sophia said. She set her tray down and then was tackled by girls. The boys were a little more professional but not as much. Almost everybody in the room knew the all-to-famous cowgirl from either coming to camp as a camper or working at Camp for a year while she was there. Then Perry walked in.

"What is this? An Abbot reunion?" Jason exclaimed. Everyone laughed as they were introduced to the oldest one in the family, Perry Abbot.

"Nice to see you too, bud. And what's this?" Perry asked, holding up Cassidy's ring and showing it to Jason. When she reached out to hug her older brother, he had spotted it. This was news to everyone but Cassidy, Chloe, Jason, and Hannah who all knew they were engaged.

"It's a ring." Jason shrugged. Perry rolled his eyes and dropped Cassidy's hand. "What does it look like to you?"

"It looks like you're engaged." Perry answered. Jason, Cassidy, and Chloe started clapping.

"Perry Abbot, the genius!" Cassidy exclaimed, motioning towards her brother. He flicked her head and sat down right between her and Jason. They both huffed and crossed their arms.

"You're not engaged." Perry told them.

"Shut up and accept the facts, Perry." Chloe sassed.

"What did y'all do to my baby sister?" Sophia gasped. She was joking though and everyone laughed. Lunch was fun but afterwards, Sophia went with Hannah and Sierra up to the barn and Perry left. After Jason, Cassidy, and Chloe finished lunch, and dessert, they went back into the kitchen to take the cooled down cookies and put them in bags. Then Jason went to get wakeboard camp from the campfire bowl while Cassidy and Chloe looked for markers and paper in the staff lounge in Cottonwood.

"Found some paper!" Chloe exclaimed. She picked up a stack of construction paper and Cassidy found a cup full of pens.

"Alrighty. Let's go!" she said. They went back into the empty cafeteria where wakeboard camp and extreme camp were. Extreme camp was on the other side of the cafeteria though, getting ready to do their activity while wakeboard camp was being told what to expect.

"Here's the paper and pens so you can start draw-ing." Jason said as Chloe and Cassidy put their stuff on a table. The campers were supposed to draw cards that they would put in the bags with the cookies. Cassidy went over to extreme camp since she was support staff for the girls' cabin and Chloe followed her.

"Hey, Cassidy." Margo said. One of the extreme camp boys walked up behind Cassidy and tapped her right shoulder while standing to the left. She looked to the left, knowing what had been played on her and glared at the boy.

"Tommy, stop it." she scolded the thirteen year old. Except it was playfull and Tommy knew it. Then his friend Brian did the same thing to Chloe. However, she was expecting it and when he tapped her shoulder, she spun around and almost kicked Brian. If he hadn't ducked, she would have hit him square in the gut.

"Whoa." Tommy said, watching Chloe. Cassidy noticed this and looked at Chloe who was glaring at Brian.

"She's like a tiny ninja. What are you doing here?" Brian asked Chloe. She looked at Cassidy and one look told her everything.

"I live here in the summer since I have family who works here." she said. Brian looked at Cassidy and so did Tommy.

"Is Cassidy your mom?" Tommy asked. Cassidy and Chloe started laughing and Jason walked over.

"What's so funny?" he asked.

"Tommy thought I was Chloe's mom." Cassidy answered.

"If you were, I was just gonna wonder who her dad was." Tommy defended. Jason got an idea in his head.

"How old do I look?" he asked. That made Chloe laugh even harder but Cassidy stopped and glared at him.

Chapter 12

After they had gotten back from delivering cookies across the lake, it was almost dinner time. Only five minutes. So wakeboard camp went back to their cabins while Cassidy, Chloe, and Jason stayed on the dock with their feet in the water. Cassidy and Chloe were laying down but Jason was sitting up.

"We should go for another boat ride." Cassidy suggested. Jason looked at his watch then back at Cassidy.

"We don't have time. Dinner's in five minutes." he told her. She propped herself up on her elbows and looked up at the cafeteria.

"How about we get our food and eat in the boat out on the lake?" she suggested. Jason shrugged and got up.

"Sure." he replied. Chloe and Cassidy jumped up and they all went up to the cafeteria. They were the first ones in line as they grabbed their food then went back down to the dock. Cassidy held Jason's food as he got three life jackets and the keys to the boat. Then they all got in, Chloe unhooked them from the dock, and they drove away. Once they were further out in the lake, Jason turned off the boat and they started eating dinner. "CJ, do you have your swim suit on?" he asked. Chloe shook her head.

"No. So you can't throw me out of the boat." she answered. They hung out in the boat for two hours then had to go back since Cassidy was acting in tonight's play. They took their plates back to the kitchen then made their way to the campfire bowl. Chloe sat between Ariana and Jason while Cassidy was behind the stage to get ready for her play. They sang a few songs then one of the programming staff members announced the skit that was about to begin.

After campfire, everyone went down to the beach for a half hour of just hanging out with friends. The staff had fifteen minutes to socialize then they had to go clean up. Chloe helped too and when they were done, it was almost midnight. Cassidy and Chloe fell into their hammocks and instantly fell asleep. Although, tomorrow they would have to get up early to go to a meeting and then help set up registration in the parking lot for the next camp. Well, Cassidy did. Chloe could do whatever she wanted as long as she wasn't in anyone's way.

"What do you want for lunch?" Chloe asked Cassidy. Cassidy was rushing to get down to her meeting soon and would miss lunch but didn't have the time to stop by the kitchen and rummage in the huge walk-in fridge. So Chloe was going to get her lunch.

"If there's any left over potatoes and gravy I'd like that. If not, there's probably still pizza from last night or steal Jason's Jamba juice." Cassidy answered. She rushed out the door and Chloe walked up to the cafeteria. She saw Asher, Sierra's best friend and Christian's brother, working in the office so she told him she was going to look in the fridge for lunch.

"Okay. If Cassidy wants, we still have a little potatoes and gravy left, saved just for her. I don't know if you'll like anything in there though. There's not a lot of left overs." Asher told her.

"Okay. Then I'll just steal Jason's Jamba juice." Chloe replied. She got the container of potatoes out then got the gravy and put the potatoes in a bowl followed by gravy dumped on top. She grabbed Cassidy a spoon, said goodbye to Asher, then went into Cottonwood where Cassidy was talking with a few other staff members about something.

"Sid!" she said. Cassidy spun around and smiled.

"Yummy. Thank you, CJ." she replied. Chloe handed her the bowl and went into the small fridge. She took Jason's Jamba juice out and walked out of Cottonwood and down to the dock where the waterfront staff where setting up for swim tests. Cassidy would usually be down with them but she was filling in for Margo as a counselor for a few days since Margo got sick.

"Hey, Jason." Chloe said, walking over to him.

"Hey. Wait, is that my Jamba juice? That was for Cassidy." he told her.

"I know. She said I could have it for lunch." she replied.

Chapter 13

That afternoon, registration started. The wranglers were around camp, either helping up at the barn with hay or running around camp helping set up for that night. Cassidy was up at the cabins getting campers brought to her and Chloe was on the dock with Jason and the other waterfront staff set up for swim tests. Chloe had a blue band on, as did all the water front staff and counselors, to show that she could swim but wasn't a camper.

"CJ, go run this up to Cassidy and Arianna." Shannon said, handing Chloe a sheet of paper. It had the class schedules on it for when they needed lifeguards and who was assigned when. Chloe took both sheets and went up to the cabins. On the way up, she ran into Arianna.

"Ari! Here, this is the lifeguard schedule Shannon wanted me to give you." she said. Arianna took and skimmed through it.

"Thanks, Chloe." she said. She ran down to the office while Chloe continued to the cabins. She climbed the stairs to the second floor then turned to find her sister talking to a parent. At least that's what she assumed she was doing. Three girls who looked as if they knew each other were talking inside the cabin on a bed and another girl was with her dad and mom being introduced to some of the other girls.

"Oh! Are you a camper here too?" a mother asked Chloe. Chloe shook her head.

"No. But I'm a junior staff member. What do you need?" she replied. The mom looked confused.

"I was just wondering what I do with this." the mom said. She held a piece of paper out she got at the beginning of registration. Chloe skimmed over it, looking for any allergies but there was none.

"As long as she's not allerigc to anything, you can keep it." she answered. The mom nodded, hugged her daughter, then left. Chloe went over to Cassidy and the man she was talking to. He had a little girl on his leg and another girl standing beside him which indicated he was a dad. But he must be divorced because he was attempting to flirt with Cassidy. Chloe thought she could use some help so she went over in the middle of their conversation and tried something new. "Hey, mom!" she smiled. Cassidy's eyes said thank you even though she tried not to show the man.

"Hey. What's this?" Cassidy asked, taking the schedule from Chloe.

"The schedule. Shannon wanted to give it to you. And daddy says you can come down anytime with your cabin." Chloe answered.

"Well, I've got her from here." Cassidy told the dad. He nodded, looking sad and left his daughter.

"Is she your daughter?" the girl asked.

"No. She's my sister." Cassidy answered as Chloe ran back down to the docks. When she arrived, she saw Jason and suddenly felt like she should tell him what happened with Cassidy. But something else told her it might not rub well with him. So she tried to avoid him, to no luck.

"CJ, where's my phone?" he asked.

"I don't know." she shortly answered. She quickly walked away from him but he followed her, instantly knowing something was up. He grabbed her arm and picked her up so she couldn't run away. She glared at him and he smiled.

"Whatcha hiding in that thing you call a brain?" he said.

"Nothing!" she exclaimed. He gave her a look and she sighed. "Let me down first." she said. He set her down and she dove into the water. It was a good thing she was wearing her swim suit with shorts so she didn't ruin her clothes.

"Chloe Jenessa Maureen Abbot!" Jason yelled, using her full name. Chloe resurfaced and glared at him. She had heard him yelling and wasn't happy with him. She didn't liked her middle names Jenessa and Maureen and he knew that.

"Just ask Cassidy but don't let her know I told you to." she replied before climbing out and going with Will to tell the new campers the dock rules. They went to the grass beside the beach and over to the guys' cabin that had arrived. Chloe quickly tied her wet hair into a bun then stood beside Will.

"Alright boys, we'll just tell you the dock rules before going to take our swim tests. My name's Will and this is Chloe. We'll be here all week so if you have any questions, we'll be on the dock." Will said. Then he looked at Chloe who had stolen Jason's cowboy hat as she had walked behind Will. "Well, I will. I don't know about Chloe." he finished.

"Shut up." Chloe told him. This was teen camp, meaning everyone at this camp was somewhere between fourteen and sixteen. Older than her no matter what so she would just have to hide her age. "So first rule, no running on the dock. See the boy running this way, yeah, don't do that." she instructed, pointing at Jason who was running her way. When he arrived, he grabbed Chloe and pulled her aside.

"What happened to Cassidy?" he demanded.

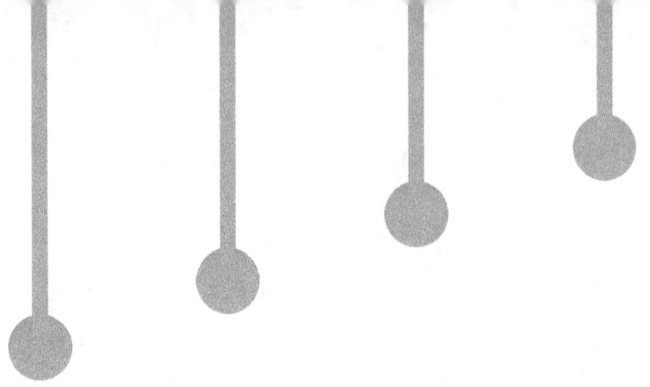

Chapter 14

ill continued the rules with the boys while Jason and Chloe argued a couple feet away.

"Nothing happened. You just have to talk to her. It was one of the parents." Chloe told him.

"Just tell me." he said.

"No! Talk to Cassidy." she stubbornly said. She went back over to Will and stood beside him. Jason went back onto the dock and Chloe stayed with Will.

"How old are you?" one of the boys asked. He looked sixteen and like he would be trouble. That's just what they wanted. More trouble.

"By camp rules, I'm not allowed to tell you my age." Will answered. Then the boy looked at Chloe.

"What about her? She's not old enough to be a staff member." he replied. Chloe looked up, her eyes piercing through the boys in a demanding matter. She could be very commanding and scary sometimes for a thirteen year old girl.

"That isn't your business, is it. I'm here telling you the rules so I must have some authority from somewhere." she replied. Will give her a hidden high five before they went onto the dock. The boys started their swim test and another cabin of girls came so Chloe and Will did the same thing with them. It went fine after that until Cassidy's cabin came. When she walked onto the dock by Jason and Chloe, she wasn't expected to be interregated.

"How did drop off go?" Jason asked her.

"Fine. Why?" she replied. He never asked about pick up and drop off so this was weird.

"I was just wondering. You never know with those parents." he said. Cassidy didn't know how he knew but when it clicked, Chloe was already sneaking away.

"Chloe!" she snapped.

"I didn't tell him! He figured it out on his own." Chloe huffed.

"Not the entire story." Jason said. Cassidy crossed her arms and glared at her sister and fiance. When she knew she had no other option, she sighed and told Jason what happened.

"There was just this dad who came to drop off his kid and he started flirting with me. Nothing bad happened though because Chloe came up and called me mom and you dad." Cassidy told him.

"Thank you. And I'm sorry." Jason replied. Cassidy took her girls back to the cabin to wait until dinner was ready. Jason and Chloe finished swim tests then went up to the cafeteria only to find Cassidy's table full of girls with no more room. However, Jason had other ideas. Since Arianna was using a seat at Cassidy's table, he talked to her. Arianna agreed to move seats so that he could sit at the table instead.

"Where do I sit?" Chloe asked.

"With Ari." Jason answered.

"Or I could sit on you." she suggested. Jason came back and took Arianna's seat and tried to scoot in before Chloe could sit on him but she made it there first.

"Hey, Chloe." Cassidy said.

"Hey! I'm here too, you know." Jason stated.

"I'm well aware of that." Cassidy replied. Cassidy introduced all the girls to Chloe and Chloe to all the girls. Jason had to butt in though because Cassidy was ignoring him.

"Cassidy, I said I was sorry." he said.

"I'll talk to you later." she shortly told him. During campfire, Chloe saw Cassidy and Jason sneak away and around the corner to talk. She couldn't quite tell what was going on but when she saw them come back, they looked like everything had worked out. Which was good because this is where the story ends. With everything on the right track and going good.

About the Author

Liz Mac is from North Idaho who spends a majority of her time writing books for children. She loves to read and always has since she was a little girl. Liz has a passion for horses and loves riding them with her friends She's the oldest in her family with a younger sister. She grew up skiing but eventually changed to snowboarding and has been ever since.